A Hundred and One
Daffodils

MALACHY DOYLE

ILLUSTRATED BY DENISE HUGHES

BLOOMSBURY EDUCATION

LONDON OXFORD NEW YORK NEW DELHI SYDNEY

For Nuala – MD.

BLOOMSBURY EDUCATION
Bloomsbury Publishing Plc
50 Bedford Square, London, WC1B 3DP, UK
29 Earlsfort Terrace, Dublin 2, Ireland

BLOOMSBURY, BLOOMSBURY EDUCATION and the Diana logo
are trademarks of Bloomsbury Publishing Plc

First published in Great Britain in 2021 by Bloomsbury Publishing Plc

A catalogue record for this book is available from the British Library

ISBN: PB: 978-1-4729-8885-0; ePDF: 978-1-4729-8888-1; ePub: 978-1-4729-8889-8;
enhanced ePub: 978-1-4729-8886-7

2 4 6 8 10 9 7 5 3 1

Printed and bound in China by Leo Paper Products, Heshan, Guangdong

MIX
Paper from
responsible sources
FSC
www.fsc.org   FSC® C020056

All papers used by Bloomsbury Publishing Plc are natural, recyclable products from wood
grown in well managed forests and other sources. The manufacturing processes conform to the
environmental regulations of the country of origin

To find out more about our authors and books visit www.bloomsbury.com
and sign up for our newsletters

Chapter One

Dusty woke from a deep sleep. Someone was prodding her with his paw. Opening her eyes, she saw that it was her dad.

"Come and see if you can find your very first daffodil!" he was saying. "It's a bright sunny morning and they're just starting to open. I can smell them!"
"A daffodil?" Dusty yawned. "What's a daffodil?"
She sniffed. And sniffed again.

4

"There is a funny smell," she said, twitching her nose.

"It's the daffodils!" said her dad.

"Come and see!"

He led her up and out of their den, and over to a beautiful yellow flower.

"Your very first one!" he said to
Dusty. "I remember when I was nearly
a year old, just like you are now," he
told her, as she snuggled up next to
him. "Ma Fox took me up and out of
the foxhole, and showed me my very
first daffodil…"

"Just like me and you, today!"
said Dusty.
Her dad went on to say how Ma Fox
had told him there'd be more and
more opening all the time. She'd said
to count them, and when he got to a
hundred and one, it meant it was the
first day of springtime.

"What's springtime?" Dusty asked him. "The best time of the year!" said her dad. "It's when the cold dark days of winter are finally over and everything starts growing again. And on the first day of springtime all the animals have a big party."

"Oh!" said Dusty, who loved parties.
"So did you find them all?"
"Oh yes," said her dad. "My friends and
I went on a daffodil hunt, and we didn't
rest till we found a hundred and one!"
"And did you have a party?"

"Oh yes. That year, and every year after, till I was a proper grown-up fox."

So Dusty decided, there and then, to see if she could find a hundred and one daffodils. Because then it'd be the first day of springtime and she could have a great big party!

Chapter Two

Dusty ran off to find her best friend, Mabel the mole. "The daffodils are coming! The daffodils are coming!" she cried. "What's a daffodil?" said the little mole, peeping out from under the grass.

"It's the prettiest big yellow flower,"
Dusty told her. "And the world's full of
them in springtime."
She led Mabel back to the first
opening daffodil – the one her dad had
shown her. "Soon there'll be lots and
lots of them, all over the place!"

"Will there be a hundred?" asked Mabel.

"More!" said Dusty.

"A thousand?"

"There'll be squillions!" cried Dusty.

"Don't you remember last spring, Mabel?"

"I don't think I was born then," said the little mole.

"Oh," said Dusty. "Well, neither was I – but that's when they come out. All we have to do is find a hundred and one. Then it'll be springtime, and we'll have a great big party!"

They agreed that Dusty would do the searching, because she was faster and her eyes were sharper. And Mabel would do all the counting.

So off they went,
through the fields and
the forest, till at the end
of the day Dusty said,
"How many's that?"

"Oh," said Mabel. "Oh dear…" She couldn't remember!

"You silly mole!" said Dusty, crossly. "Now we'll have to start all over again tomorrow. Spring will never come at this rate. And we'll never have a party!"

Mabel's eyes filled with big wet mole tears, and she slunk off quietly into the undergrowth.

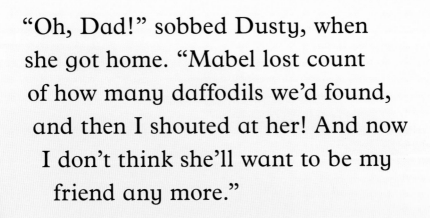

"Oh, Dad!" sobbed Dusty, when
she got home. "Mabel lost count
of how many daffodils we'd found,
and then I shouted at her! And now
I don't think she'll want to be my
friend any more."

"Tomorrow's a new day," said her father, giving her a cuddle. "If you tell Mabel, the next time you see her, that you're sorry for being cross, I'm sure she'll still be your friend."

Chapter Three

But the next day there was no sign of Mabel. No sign of her at all. "Oh dear," Dusty sighed. "I'll have to find the daffodils all by myself."

She ran to where she'd seen her
first open daffodil and there were
three more beside it!
"*Four!*" she yelled, excitedly.

She charged all about, and there was
another daffodil... and another...
and another.
"*Seven!*"

But then Dusty couldn't find any more. "Oh dear," she muttered. "I'll never find enough all on my own. Where's Mabel?"

Just then she heard her friend, Ricky Robin, calling to her from a tree nearby.

And when she looked over, there was another patch of daffodils, in the grass just below him!

"Oh, thank you, Ricky!" she cried. "That's *eleven!*" The little robin whistled, flying from bush to bush.

"Three more!" laughed Dusty, chasing after him. "And another two! That's *sixteen* lovely daffodils!"

At that moment, a dark cloud went over the sun. Dusty turned and ran for home, but before she could get there the rain began to fall, lightly at first, then harder and harder.

"Dad! Dad!" she cried, as she plopped down into the den. "What happens if it goes all dark and there's no sun? The flowers can't come out, can they?"
"Oh, the clouds will blow away soon," said her dad.

"And anyway, the rain will help them grow," he added.
But Dusty still felt worried, looking out at the heavy rain.

The sky got darker, the rain got heavier, and in the middle of the night a massive storm swept through the forest.

When Dusty emerged from her family's cosy den the next morning, she found broken branches, uprooted bushes, grass pulled out at the roots, and... Daffodils? Where were the daffodils? Dusty searched everywhere, but she couldn't see a single one.

She went to all the places she'd found them before, but they were either gone altogether, or bent and broken.

"I'll never find enough!" cried Dusty. "Springtime will never come!"

Chapter Four

The following morning Dusty popped out of her hole bright and early, and there was Mabel, waiting to speak to her. "I'm sorry for being silly the other day and forgetting how many daffodils we'd found," said the little mole.

"You're a very nice fox cub, Dusty, and I'm glad that you're my friend," she added.

"Well, I'm sorry for losing my temper and shouting at you," said Dusty, in return. "And I could really do with your help, after that terrible storm."

"OK," said Mabel. "Let's find some daffodils. And I promise I won't get in a muddle with the counting this time!" So the two friends set off on their search.

A lot of the daffodils were ruined, but quite a few of the ones that had been flattened by the storm had managed to stand up again. And a lot of the ones that hadn't opened yet, when Dusty had been looking the day before, were now wide to the sun.

They found twenty, thirty, forty,
fifty, sixty…
"*Seventy-one, seventy-two, seventy-three…*"
Mabel counted, as she and Dusty went
this way and that, through the fields
and the forest, until they were too tired
to continue.

"Maybe we'll find another, eh… twenty-eight, tomorrow," said Mabel, on their way home. "Then it'll be springtime!"

Chapter Five

"Right," said Dusty, when she met up with Mabel the following morning. "Let's find the last few daffodils!" So off they went together, hoppity skip. "*Seventy-nine*!" they shouted, finding another six.

They went back to the clump of willow at the edge of the wood, to check if the ones there had opened yet, and eight of them had. Then they went right to the heart of the wood, and there were four more.

"Ten to go!" cried Dusty.
"*Nine*," cried Mabel, finding one in the long grass.

"Eight, seven, six!" squeaked Dusty, spotting another three in a tangle of dead wood.

"Five, four!" laughed Mabel, peeping through the undergrowth.

"Three!" cried Dusty, finding another one, all alone in a clearing. "And *two!*" But then their luck ran out. They couldn't find any more, no matter how hard they looked.

"Ricky!" cried Dusty, spotting her little friend, the robin. "Have you seen any new daffodils? We only need another two."

"We've counted that one before," said Mabel, as Ricky led them to one.

"No, we haven't."

"Yes, we have."

"Well, *that's* a new one!" cried Dusty, as Ricky landed on a bush just above a single daffodil. "So there's only one more to go!"

Ricky took off again, leading them all the way through the wood, until they came to a meadow on the other side.

"Over here!" Ricky called, from beyond the trees.

"You found it!" yelled Dusty, bounding through the forest, following the sound of Ricky's voice. "That's *a hundred and one!*" yelled Dusty. *"It's springtime!"*

Chapter Six

Dusty and Mabel ran as fast as they could towards the edge of the forest. And who did they find when they emerged into the sunshiny meadow beyond?

Not just Ricky, but Dusty's dad and mum and her younger brothers and sisters, Mabel's whole family, and all their friends, too.

And all around them, lit by the pinky purple light of the setting sun, was a whole meadow full of daffodils.
"Squillions of them!" squeaked Dusty.
"Well done, Dusty!" cried her dad.
"Yes, well done, Dusty and Mabel!" cried everyone.

"And Ricky!" said Dusty. "Well done,
Ricky, too!"
And there, spread out on tree stumps,
near the edge of the forest,
was a huge…

"Feast!" cried Dusty. "A springtime feast!"

There was lots and lots of lovely food – nuts and seeds and lettuce and fruit. All of Dusty and Mabel's favourite treats.

In fact, there was everything Dusty and her friends could possibly want for a wonderful party in the spring evening sunshine.

"How did you do it, Mum and Dad?" said Dusty, amazed. "How did you know where we'd be?"

Her mum smiled up at Ricky Robin.
"A little birdy told me," she said.
So they ate and they drank till their
tummies were full.
Then they danced and they skipped,
in and out of the daffodils, in and out

of the trees, till they'd room to eat and
drink a little more.
And then they sang and told stories,
as the bright spring moon rose over
the treetops and bathed them all in its
warm yellow light.

"Yellow flowers, yellow moon," said Dusty, happily. And it was the last thing she said, because with that she fell into the deepest of deepest sleeps. And her dad carried her home.